Prayers for an Angel
By Dr. Shavon Leach

Thoughts On Prayers for an Angel

"I love the depth of scripture you include in the chapters. I also love how you share that healing is a gradual process. Many people think healing is instant, especially when we are in Christ."
~Pastor Jenelle Thompson

"I actually loved chapter 10 because of the transformation: if God could do it for Dallas, one who had a bitter heart, he surely can do it for us. Called out to God, God answered by the way of an angel called Lena. His heart was open to learn and obey in surrender."
~Coach K Angela Lee

"Dr. Vonie has been gifted by God as a writer who inspires others through words on a page."
~Coach Lissa Figgins

"Prayers for an Angel is a great series of short reads. The stories are short and simple, but each carries a significant amount of knowledge that can be easily applied to personal life. It's a very easy and relatable read."
~Coach Tracy Hinnant

"I love how each story is relatable and speaks to every situation we face today. I love how the angel works with each character according to their need, helping them turn back to God and giving them practical life application through meditating on scripture and prayer."
~Coach Leteisha Tate

Table of Contents

INTRODUCTION

Prayers for an Angel is a collection of short Christian fiction stories. The angel and some of its abilities were created for this book. Each story contains biblical scripture from the Holy Bible.

The angel in this book represents God's love, compassion, and healing mercies. *Prayers for an Angel* explores the guiding power of angels, the transformative power of prayer, and the ability to make it through anything. These stories are designed to be a source of strength, inviting you to explore the Word and forge a deeper connection with God.

As you journey through the pages of *Prayers for an Angel*, may you find peace, guidance, healing, and strength to navigate life's challenges. I hope these stories resonate with your heart and draw you closer to God, Our Father.

Prayers for an Angel by Dr. Shavon Leach

CHAPTER 1: The Creation of Lena

The Creation of Lena

God observed the world below with a heavy heart. He watched as humanity struggled with physical, emotional, and mental ailments that tore at the fabric of their lives. People across the land suffered from sickness, pain, and heartache, desperately seeking comfort. God, in His infinite wisdom, recognized that the world needed a powerful source of hope and healing.

God envisioned an Angel, a divine being with a gentle heart and boundless compassion, who would guide humanity toward healing and understanding and to Him. This vision grew into a passionate gift for the world. God created a soul that shimmered with exquisite beauty on the dawn of a new day. He gathered the purest elements of unmatched benevolence, the light of hope, the essence of compassion, and the unwavering strength of resilience. God carefully combined these elements with a divine strategy.

God breathed life into the soul, and from it emerged Lena, the Angel of Healing. She was a breathtaking sight, with white, purple, and gold wings that stretched wide, radiant, and strong. Her eyes shined like the stars in the night's sky, reflecting the vast spectrum of human emotions. Her shiny black hair flowed like a gentle river, symbolizing the constant flow of God-given healing.

God gave Lena the divine gifts of empathy, wisdom, and healing. She could listen to the world's suffering and understand the depths of each person's pain. She would use her God-given wisdom to guide the world toward God's healing and provide comfort in their darkest hours. Her touch alone could mend broken bones, heal wounded hearts, and soothe the most tormented souls.

Lena, the Angel of Healing, descended upon the world, bringing power that touched every corner of the earth. She traveled the land as God instructed. With Lena's guidance granted to her by God, anyone who had once been consumed by pain and sorrow found comfort; but most importantly, Lena restored faith in God.

As the world began to heal, the people rejoiced and thanked God for the gift of Lena. The Angel of Healing continued her divine mission, her heart swelling with love and gratitude for the opportunity to serve God and humanity. And so it was that Lena, became a symbol of hope and comfort for all who sought her aid.

CHAPTER 2: The Weight of Expectations

Landon was born into the humble home of the Grimes family. Their family was religious, with generations of pastors and believers leading the way to the Lord's grace. Landon was the eldest of five children, and from the moment his siblings were born, a great weight was placed upon his shoulders. Evangeline Grimes, Landon's mother, saw her children as the ultimate blessing.

However, she held Landon to an impossible standard, believing that God ordained him to be the protector and spiritual guide for his younger siblings as the eldest. "Landon," she said, "The Lord has chosen you to shepherd your brothers and sisters through life. Your sacred duty is to keep them safe and close to God."

Landon took this burden seriously, but deep within him, it planted the seeds of relentless anxiety. He was never at ease. He felt responsible for every misstep his siblings took. He would lie awake at night, his heart racing as he thought about the immense task he had been given. The pressure to be a perfect example was suffocating, and every time he felt he could not measure up to his mother's expectations, his anxiety grew even more.

As the years passed, Landon sought refuge in his faith and found hope in the sacred scriptures of God's word. He felt a calling to serve God as a pastor, and after years of study and devotion, he stepped into his role as pastor at The Church of Divine Harmony. He built a small church with a loving congregation. His sermons were passionate and inspiring, and he felt a great purpose in spreading God's word.

But the anxiety that haunted him since childhood never left. It lingered in the back of his mind, whispering doubts and fears into his thoughts. As a pastor, Landon felt a newfound responsibility to his congregation, and the pressure of guiding them on the path to salvation weighed heavily on him. He constantly questioned whether he was doing enough or if he was leading them astray, and the anxiety grew until it became a constant companion.

CHAPTER 3: Landon's Cry

Landon Grimes was a great man of faith and a dedicated pastor. Landon was a true shepherd. He was unwavering in his walk, delivering sermons filled with truth, hope, and compassion. He counseled the congregation and community members on forgiveness, salvation, and how to be Christ-like. Landon had a gift of connecting with people, but deep within, he was struggling. The constant fear and worry had begun to wear him down, leaving him doubting his abilities as a pastor and servant of God.

Anxiety

Despite his success as a pastor, Landon continued to struggle with crippling anxiety that threatened to consume him. One night, Landon's anxiety reached a new level of intensity. He could not sleep and paced through his home. He felt the weight of the world on his shoulders. He began to feel a familiar pressure from childhood rise in him. Amid his anxiety attack, Landon remembered that he could always find peace at The Church of Divine Harmony.

So, he went to church.

Landon barely made it to the altar when he dropped to his knees with tears streaming down his face. Landon spent hours praising and worshiping God for how far he had come and the impact God allowed him to make. He sat in silence for a few moments, then prayed,

"Our Father whom art in Heaven hollowed be thy name. I need help. I need strength and guidance. I am struggling, and I feel like I am drowning in fear and worry. I need help letting go. Please, Father, send divine intervention to help me overcome my anxiety. Send me an Angel. In Jesus name, Amen."

London's prayer echoed through the empty church. At that moment, the church radiated with a bright light, the walls trembled, and he was momentarily blinded. The doors of the church flew open. As the light began to dim, Landon was face to face with an Angel. He dropped to his knees again.

"Fear not," the Angel said. "I am Lena, an Angel sent by God to help you heal from your anxiety."

Wasting no time, Lena began working with Landon immediately. To help him confront his anxiety and build deeper faith in God, Lena led

Landon through scripture study, meditation, and holographic simulation. "Landon, when you regularly reflect and meditate on God's word it will help you to better navigate challenging situations without becoming overwhelmed by anxiety. You will be able to understand the Word of God, speak truth to anxiety, and cast it down," Lena shared.

"Now, let's look at several pieces of scripture. *Philippians 4:6-7 says, "Be anxious for nothing, but in everything by prayer and supplication, with thanksgiving, let your requests be made known to God; and the peace of God, which surpasses all understanding, will guard your hearts and minds through Christ Jesus."* Your anxiety comes from uncertainty and a lack of control. To truly heal from anxiety, you must learn to let go of those very things. As you pray, be thankful from where God has brought you, and as you trust God, he will give you peace that will guard and protect you.

1 Peter 5:7 says, *"casting all your care upon Him, for He cares for you."* God loves you. He wants you to give Him all of your worries, all of your doubts, and all of the things that weigh you down.

Psalm 94:19 *"In the multitude of my anxieties within me, Your comforts delight my soul."* When inner turmoil arises, God is able to give you guidance and reassurance.

Isaiah 41:10 *"Fear not, for I am with you; Be not dismayed, for I am your God. I will strengthen you, Yes, I will help you, I will uphold you with My righteous right hand."* God is with you. There is no need to be afraid, panicked, or discouraged. God promises to strengthen you with all of His might.

Matthew 6:34 *"Therefore do not worry about tomorrow, for tomorrow will worry about its own things. Sufficient for the day is its own trouble."* Take each moment one step at a time. Do not add today's weight to tomorrow's plate. Each day has its own challenges. Focus on your here and now.

Landon, meditate on these scriptures and remember that God is always with you, ready to support and guide you through challenging times. Cast your anxieties upon Him and find healing in His eternal love and care for you," Lena said.

Lena stayed with Landon as he worked to overcome anxiety. While Landon spent time meditating on God's word, Lena wrapped her wings around him and prayed. Once Landon mastered his ability to meditate on God's word and let go of uncertainty and control, God granted Lena the power to use holographic simulation. Lena and Landon appeared as faded images as they visited the moment his anxiety began and several other memories that contributed to his anxiety. They watched in silence. Landon's eyes filled with tears because he remembered the strain he felt. After revisiting several memories, they returned to their present moment. Landon took a deep breath and looked at Lena with freedom in his eyes; then Lena began to heal him.

Landon paused momentarily, then said, "This is the first time in a long time I've felt light and free."

"You were carrying a load never meant for you. God sent His son, Jesus Christ, a long time ago to carry everyone's load." Lena continued to minister to Landon, and he found strength and total healing in God; when her time with Landon was done, God sent Lena to her next assignment.

ETHAN & LILLY'S Story CHAPTER 4: Love
Rekindled

Love Rekindled

Ethan and Lilly have been married for 15 years. They have three children: Nolan, Krystal, and Benjamin. Nolan is eleven years old and wants to be an astronaut when he grows up. Krystal is eight and wants to own her a hotel. Benjamin is three years old. He is Ethan and Lilly's surprise child. Ethan is a brain surgeon and a local Social Services Department Medical Consultant. Ethan spends a portion of his days off visiting the sick and shut-ins who are medically incapable of traveling to their doctors' appointments. Lilly owns a bakery specializing in elegant and theatrical cakes for children. She is one of the most requested bakers in her state. People travel from all over the world to purchase her baked goods.

Ethan and Lilly love each other very much. But over time, the weight of marriage, work, and children's schedules put pressure on their marriage. They lost track of each other and found it harder to communicate with each passing day. Because of their lack of communication, Ethan and Lilly began to argue about everything. Even the simplest conversations turned into heated discussions. One night, during an argument, Lilly became so enraged and fed up that she yelled, "I want a divorce!" That statement stopped Ethan in his tracks. Lilly walked past Ethan, staring at him as she entered the guest room and slammed the door.

Ethan walked into their bedroom and sat in disbelief on the edge of the bed. He laid his face in his hands and began to cry. He never imagined that he would ever hear those words. Ethan tossed and turned all night, replaying the same statement over and over. The following day, he tried to speak to Lilly, but she ignored him. Three months passed, and communication didn't change. Ethan and Lilly only spoke to discuss the children's schedules. Ethan worried Lilly's cold heart would lead to their separation. One morning before work, Ethan finally asked Lilly, "Where did we go wrong?" Lilly momentarily stopped and took a deep breath, "Over time, we grew apart. Some things don't last forever."

Ethan looked at Lilly and asked, "What is wrong with you? Is there a problem? Why don't you want this marriage to work? I understand we lost ourselves along the way, but that does not mean we give up. Giving up was not in the vows that we made to each other. Don't those mean anything to you?"

Lilly stopped at the bedroom door as she was leaving, "Why do you care now? What about when I asked you and begged you to talk and get help to get our marriage and communication back on track, and you ignored me? And now you want to try to talk? I have nothing else to say."

"I'm sorry," Ethan yelled as Lilly walked away. Ethan went to work that day and pretended like nothing was wrong. By the night's end, Ethan was so tired and worn out from all the acting that he dropped to the floor in his office and began to cry. He sat there and cried for an hour.

Ethan prayed to God for the first time in a long time,

> *"Heavenly Father, I know it has been a long time since I've spoken to You. And I know that I do not deserve or even have the right to come to You and ask You for anything. Especially since I've ignored You and my wife for so long. Lord, I do not want to lose my wife. I do not want to lose my family. God, please send someone to help me and my wife get back to us, but most importantly, Lord, help us get back to You. In Jesus name, Amen."*

It was then that Ethan was sucked into a warm and brilliant light. He appeared in his bedroom next to his wife. They both looked at each other curiously. "What is happening?" Lilly asked. Ethan's eyes widened as he saw the same warm and brilliant light reappear.

"Fear not," a soothing voice said.

"My name is Lena, and I am an Angel of the Lord. Ethan, the Lord has heard your cries and sent me to help you and Lilly to become one again."

Lilly looked at Ethan with a slight look of hope in her eyes. Lena began working with Ethan and Lilly immediately. Once again, God granted Lena the ability to use holographic simulation to help Ethan and Lilly go back in time to the moment they first laid eyes on each other. Ethan and Lilly were so busy on their cell phones that they walked right into each other, and dropped their phones.

"I'm so sorry," they each said. Ethan looked up and saw the most beautiful woman he had ever seen. Her eyes sparkled like a stream at night in the moonlight. When he saw her, his mind was instantly sent on a roller coaster of future visions of love, peacefulness, and hope. When Lilly looked up, she stopped breathing for a moment. She had never seen anyone so breathtaking. Her mind was immediately sent down the waterfall of life, healing, and togetherness. Ethan and Lilly watched their past selves fall in love at first sight.

Over the years, they lost sight of each other and the visions that God had given them for how their lives were supposed to be and what they were supposed to create. Tears once again filled both of their eyes. They were brought to another memory of their first dance at their wedding: Lilly wore a long, beautiful white gown covered in pearls and lavender glitter. Her hair was in a curly updo, and she wore a veil that trailed 3 feet behind her. Ethan wore a navy tuxedo with a white shirt, shiny black shoes, and a small lavender handkerchief in his topcoat pocket. Ethan and Lilly watched themselves dancing like no one else was around. They remembered how their hearts used to beat as one and how that oneness felt under God.

Lena pulled Ethan and Lilly back to their bedroom and began working with them.

"First, I would like to remind both of you about the foundation of your marriage. Ephesians 5:31 says, *"For this reason a man shall leave his father and mother and be joined to his wife, and the two shall become one flesh."* You two have been joined together as one. One is a deep connection that binds you two in spirit. You cannot operate as one when either of you is unheard and distant. It is essential to remember that as you face any difficulty."

Lena continued, "One important aspect of a healthy marriage is effective communication. Ephesians 4:26-27 states, *"Be angry, and do not sin: do not let the sun go down on your wrath, nor give place to the devil."* This scripture reminds both of you to express your feelings and emotions in a healthy and constructive way. When you are upset with one another, communicate openly and honestly without allowing resentment to fester. When tensions are high, take a few moments to calm down and get back together that same day to resolve the matter at hand. If you allow your anger to take root, you allow the enemy to come in and tear your marriage apart."

Lena spent several months with Ethan and Lilly, encouraging them and helping them find strength in God, the Word, and each other. Lena continued to remind them of various aspects of marriage. "Remember to prioritize your relationship with God. Ecclesiastes 4:12 says, *"Though one may be overpowered by another, two can withstand him. And a threefold cord is not quickly broken."* In this passage, the cord of three strands refers to a marriage where both partners are connected to God. A marriage grounded in God is more resilient and better equipped to face life's challenges.

Another critical component of a strong marriage is love. 1 Corinthians 13:4-8 states, *"Love suffers long and is kind; love does not envy; love does not parade itself, is not puffed up; does not behave rudely, does not seek its own, is not provoked, thinks no evil; does not rejoice in iniquity, but rejoices in the truth; bears all things, believes all things, hopes all things, endures all things. Love never fails."*

Marriage is hard, and it takes a lot of work. You must be patient, enduring and tolerating delay, trouble, or suffering without becoming annoyed or giving up. You must be kind, continuously being caring, and compassionate. Many times, people allow their insecurities to turn into envy. Being envious is dangerous. Genuine love does not involve self-promotion, arrogance, or an inflated sense of self-importance. It's about being humble and modest and recognizing that love is not an opportunity to elevate oneself above the other. Boastfulness in marriage causes a great disconnect from each other. You cannot love when focused on the person in the mirror. Provoked is not a verb that should be associated with marriage. When you provoke your spouse, you treat them disrespectfully, degrade them, or devalue their worth. That is not marriage.

Love is about giving, not just receiving, and it prioritizes the needs and desires of the other person. Do not hold on to the things that were done wrong. Give each other the opportunity to grow and improve without being defined by past mistakes. You should not find joy when either of you sins or stumbles. Your spouse's downfall should not make you gloat. As Christ-like individuals, your first instinct should be to pray for one another."

Lena paused and looked at Ethan and Lilly. They had a look of conviction on their faces. They were guilty of all of those things.

Lena continued, "While the truth may not always be easy to hear, it is important to hear. You must constantly guard each other's well-being. You must trust in love. You should always have faith in each other. Perseverance can be hard, but you should always show up for each other with a positive attitude, even in the face of adversity, and continue to move forward even when times are hard. Perseverance is important because it ensures that failure is not an option. Loving like this ensures that love does not fail.

Lastly, forgiveness is so important in marriage. Colossians 3:13 says, *"bearing with one another, and forgiving one another, if anyone has a complaint against another; even as Christ forgave you, so you also must do."* Remember that both of you are imperfect and will make mistakes. Just as God forgives you, you must extend that same forgiveness to one another."

Lena wrapped Ethan and Lilly in her wings and prayed for them. When Lena's time with them was over, she left them with one last piece of advice: "I encourage both of you to pray and read scripture together, seeking God's guidance for your marriage daily. With His help, you can overcome any struggle you may face.

From that moment on, Ethan and Lilly became one again, and their love was rekindled.

ELISE'S STORY CHAPTER 5: Running To Christ

Running To Christ

By the age of 25, Elise was tired of running. She ran away from everything. By the age of ten, She had run away from every foster home she lived in. When she was five, she ran away from the Smiths. They were abusive and took foster children for the benefits and money. Elise ran away several times before her caseworker placed her in another home.

The Perkins' house was the final home she stayed in. Elise lived there for a couple of years. The Perkins seemed to be a decent family for a while until they started having people over. Elise ran away because she did not like the strange things happening. Repeatedly, the caseworker would bring Elise back. One day, Elise's caseworker switched vehicles and parked down the street from the Perkins' house, watching their every move. The Perkins, who were pharmacists, were selling prescription medication.

The caseworker tried several other homes, but nothing kept Elise in place, not even the good foster homes. The only other option Elise's caseworker had was to send her to Rita's Foster Care Group Home for Children and Teens. She could not run away from there, but it did not stop her from trying. For a while, Elise stopped. She finished middle and high school at the top of her classes. She found that she enjoyed serving others and working behind the scenes to get things done. Elise's ability to lead caught the attention of everyone who met her.

However, she struggled with anger and vulgarity.

Mr. Johnny, a mentor who volunteered at the group-home, owned Derek's Leadership Academy, where Elise received a full scholarship. She remained at the top of her class and led well. However, her anger and vulgarity prevented her from reaching her full potential. Throughout her time at Derek's Leadership Academy, many tried to talk with her about her anger and language, but none succeeded.

On the evening of graduation, Mr. Johnny and his wife took Elise to dinner to celebrate her accomplishments. While waiting for dessert, Mr. Johnny wanted to address her anger and language. He began, "Listen, Elise, we are so proud of you. You are an exceptional leader. You can think strategically and have strong decision-making skills matched with a keen sense of empathy, allowing you to understand and address the diverse needs of the people around you. When you are not acting in your anger or using offensive language, you are an amazing communicator, a key strength of a good leader. You can convey ideas and expectations. You are also a great listener and can create an inclusive environment.

But, like all leaders, there are things you need to work on as well. We can see your anger, which contributes to how you speak. Your anger and your language prevent you from stepping into rooms that God has ordained you to be in. Your anger and language will also prevent you from reaching your greatest potential as a leader. God has so much in store for you, but first, you must turn to God so that he can heal you."

Elise responded, "If God wanted me to turn to him, he shouldn't have dealt me the hand I was given."

Mr. Johnny took a deep breath and said, "The things that you have been and are currently going through are hard and challenging, but they are meant to build and prepare you for what God has in store for you and what He has created you to do. But most importantly, so He can get the glory. Listen, we are not here to throw God in your face nor to shove Christianity on you, but I am here to let you know that God has great things in store for you and that we are here to teach and to help you get to where you need to be.

The church I minister at has a Community Program Development Director position available and I think you would be a good fit. If you want the position, you will be required to attend church and change how you speak. However, you do not have to do it right away. My wife, I, and some other church mentors will help, guide, and pray with you as you elevate in your walk with Christ. The position will begin at the end of summer." When dessert finally came out, they enjoyed the rest of the evening and celebrated Elise, her accomplishments, and how far she had come in life.

Once she got home, Elise felt the desire to run, so she did. She packed her belongings and bought an airplane ticket to another state. She found an apartment and quickly settled into her new position as a waitress at a local diner.

Just before summer ended, Elise wrote a letter to Mr. Johnny and his wife, thanking them for everything they had done for her and explaining why she left, noting she was not confident that she was right for the Community Program Development Director. About a month later, she received a letter back from Mr. Johnny, and it simply read: *We will be ready for you when you're ready to return. We love you, and our prayers are with you.* Not long after that, Elise met an elderly woman she saw as a grandmother. Elise and this woman spent many hours together, discussing life, challenges, and how Christ can help her overcome them. She found herself speaking more about things that made her angry and learned to let them go. She saw herself begin to change.

One night, on her way home, Elise began to hear a voice telling her it was time to come home. The voice continued for a while, and one Saturday afternoon, while walking around her city, she heard that voice again. She felt like the voice was coming from behind her. When she turned around, she saw a church with its doors open, welcoming her to come in.

The voice continued until she sat down. Elise took a deep breath,

> *"Well, God, it is clear that You want me here for a reason, and I don't know why, and I don't know what to say. But I know that Mr. Johnny said almost two and a half years ago that You had a plan for my life, so would You help me? I don't know what I need to do. I know who Christ is, and I have accepted him as my Lord and Savior. But I do not know where to start in this walk. I know there are deeply rooted things that I have to change. So, could you send someone, a person or even an Angel, to help me? I need help to start. In Jesus name. Amen"*

A couple of days later, when Elise arrived home,

she saw the light shining under her door. She nervously opened the door and saw an Angel standing there. "Oh, my Goodness," was all that could come out of her mouth as she stood there shocked.

"Fear not. My name is Lena. I am an Angel sent by the Lord.

Lena began working with Elise that night.

"Elise, God sees that you want to change and that you want better for your life," Lena said.

Elise replied with a simple "Yes."

So, what's holding you back? Lena asked.

Elise looked down and said, "I don't know where to start."

Lena smiled and said, "Let's start by putting on your new self."

Elise smiled and walked to her closet to dig out her Bible.

Lena continued, "Colossians 3:1-17 is a great starting point. Let's look at this passage in five parts,

    1. Seek Things Above

This passage begins with an invitation to seek the things above, where Christ is seated at the right hand of God. As a believer, you are now being raised with Christ, and your life is hidden in Him. Therefore, you should always focus on heavenly things and not earthly matters. Apostle Paul is telling you that your true life is with Christ.

2. Put to Death Your Earthly Nature

As you set your heart on the things above, you must also put to death your earthly nature. Apostle Paul lists various sins humans should rid themselves of, such as fornication, uncleanness, passion, evil desire, and covetousness. He also emphasizes the importance of putting away anger, wrath, malice, blasphemy, and filthy language. These actions no longer reflect the life you will lead in Christ, and you must work hard to remove them from your life. I will help you.

3. Renew Your Mind

The process of ridding yourself of sinful behavior begins with renewing your mind. You must put on your new self, which is being renewed in knowledge after the image of God. As you grow in your understanding of God and His will for your life, you will become more like Christ.

4. Clothe Yourself in Christ

As God's chosen one, holy and beloved, you are called to clothe yourself with the virtues that reflect Christ's character. These include compassion, kindness, humility, meekness, and patience. You must also bear with others and forgive others, just as the Lord has forgiven you. Above all, you are to love everyone. Love binds everything together in God's perfect harmony.

5. Live in Peace and Gratitude

As you clothe yourself in Christ, you should also let the peace of Christ rule in your heart. This peace brings unity to the body of believers and should be a foundational part of your relationships with those around you. Whatever you do, you should do it in the name of the Lord Jesus Christ and always give thanks to God."

Elise took notes and reflected on every word the Angel of the Lord told her. Lena walked with Elise daily as she spent months on each piece, helping Elise transform into who she was called to be.

Elise learned to pray continuously because now her only interest was running to Christ. Lena spent an entire year with Elise. Once she had everything she needed to begin her new walk with Christ, Elise returned home, prepared, and graciously stepped into her role as Community Program Development

Director. Mr. Johnny, his wife, and Elise's other spiritual mentors continued to work with her to build her relationship with Christ.

Over the years, Elise continued to run to God no matter how challenging life got. Elise not only excelled as a Community Program Development Director but was also one of the greatest Evangelists of her time.

To God be the Glory.

IYA'S STORY

CHAPTER 6: The Birth of Fear

Iya's childhood was filled with the whispers of an old curse passed down through generations, a curse of failure that plagued the women in her family. It was Iya's great-grandmother, Mae, who first spoke the words of the curse to her. Mae, a stern woman with a piercing gaze, believed wholeheartedly in the curse. She was a woman who had seen her dreams wither away like the petals on a dying flower, and her bitterness had only grown over the years.

"You must know the truth, Iya. You must know about the curse. It's our legacy, my child, a legacy of failure," Mae said one fateful evening when Iya was only seven years old. They were sitting on the porch of their old, creaky house, watching the sun dip below the horizon. From that day forward, the curse took root in Iya's heart, sowing seeds of fear and self-doubt. As she grew older, the curse seemed to manifest in every aspect of her life. Her schoolwork faltered, friendships slipped away, and her dreams of a brighter future drifted further out of reach with each passing day.

Despite the darkness that enveloped her, Iya tried to push forward. She studied harder, practiced her talents, and even tried to seek comfort in new friendships. But each time she tried to break free from the chains of the curse, it seemed that failure was always waiting in the shadows, ready to pull her back into its cold embrace. As the years passed, Iya's fear of failure grew, consuming her like a raging fire. Her once vibrant spirit was now a flickering flame, barely alive amidst the darkness. It was as if the curse had become an invisible wall between her and the happiness she desperately longed for.

Iya could no longer bear the burden of the curse alone. In a moment of desperation, she abandoned her dreams and moved away.

CHAPTER 7: Journey From Fear to Faith

Iya Young, a twenty-four-year-old woman, lived a life filled with fear. Despite her charming smile and warm heart, the fear of failure, rejection, and loss overwhelmed her. She often retreated to her tiny, humble apartment, where she'd spend hours praying because her heart ached for relief from the debilitating fear that held her captive. Iya's dreams were grand, but her fear paralyzed her, preventing her from taking the first step toward realizing her God-intended purpose. She longed to make a difference in the world, to touch the hearts of those around her, and to spread the love she knew God had for everyone. Iya wanted to start a traveling Missionary Ministry called In God's Arms. Her despair grew as she felt herself drifting further from her dreams.

One night, as Iya sat in bed, she fervently prayed,

"Dear God, I know it is not in Your plan for me to live in fear. I know You have greater for my life. I know it is my fault that I have allowed fear to take over my life. I tried to control my fears, but they only controlled me in the end. God, break the control I think I need and have given to fear. I give all control and fear to You. Forgive me

After she prayed, she drifted off to sleep. A soft golden light illuminated her bedroom, and Iya was awoken. She blinked as she tried to make sense of what she was seeing. In the center of the light stood a beautiful figure, an Angel with shiny black hair and radiant purple, white, and gold wings. "I am Lena, a messenger of God," the Angel said. Her voice was soothing and filled with peace. "God sent me to help guide you in overcoming your fears so you can fulfill your God-intended purpose." Tears filled Iya's eyes as she realized her prayers had been answered. Lena gently smiled, and they began their journey together.

Over the weeks that followed, Lena shared scriptures with Iya to help her confront and heal her fears. They studied Psalm 34:4, where David wrote, *"I sought the Lord, and He heard me, And delivered me from all my fears."* Iya began to understand that all she had to do was call on God, and he would help her. She realized she lacked confidence that God would be there for her.

Another verse that resonated with Iya was Joshua 1:9, "*Have I not commanded you? Be strong and of good courage; do not be afraid, nor be dismayed, for the Lord your God is with you wherever you go.*" Iya's heart swelled with hope as she embraced the words of the scripture, allowing them to seep into her soul and strengthen her spirit.

Lena visited Iya frequently. She continued to teach her valuable lessons about overcoming fear through scripture, prayer, and action. There was one scripture that Iya struggled with 2 Timothy 1:7, "*For God has not given us a spirit of fear, but of power and of love and of a sound mind.*" She struggled with this verse because fear existed in her family long before she was born. Iya shared with Lena how fear has crippled her family for generations.

Iya asked Lena, "Why would God allow fear to destroy my entire family?"

Lena looked at Iya and replied, "God does not give anyone fear. He does not allow fear to do anything to anyone because He has not given fear to anyone. God was providing an opportunity for someone in your family, which created fear in them, and instead of doing what God told them to do despite their discomfort, they allowed what they felt on the inside to stop them. Instead, they spread that same fear throughout the generations."

Iya sat in confusion for a while, then said, "I inherited this fear?! Someone was that scared?" She questioned. "So, instead of facing their fear, they passed it along? I feel so betrayed by my family."

Iya spent a few moments in silence, then said, "This fear ends with me!" Lena went on to share more scriptures with Iya. Lena watched Iya as she continued to meditate on the scriptures. Lena laid her hand on Iya's shoulder. Iya felt her fears melt away as if a heavy burden was being lifted from her soul.

She spent her days learning from Lena and practicing the lessons she taught her. Iya's confidence grew, and she understood God's love was more powerful than any fear. As Iya continued to grow in faith and conquer her fears, she found herself eager to embrace the life God had planned for her; Iya decided it was time to step into God's true plans for her life. Iya planned a day to volunteer at a local homeless shelter; she knew this would be a great way to prepare her for ministry.

For a moment, Iya could feel fear trying to re-enter

her mind. She quickly reflected again on Joshua 1:9, *"Be strong and of good courage; do not be afraid, nor be dismayed, for the Lord your God is with you wherever you go."* Iya took a deep breath and walked through the doors. As she served meals and spoke with the men and women who lived there, she realized she was no longer afraid.

Every Saturday morning, Iya went and served at the homeless shelter. After a few months, Iya started a small group for the men and women at the homeless shelter. She helped them overcome fear and much more, just as Lena had done with her. They prayed, studied the Bible, and journaled with God. Iya became an inspiration to those around her.

Ten years later, Iya started *In God's Arms Missionary Ministries.* Over the years, she touched the hearts of many and made a difference in the world, just as she'd always dreamt.

OSCAR'S STORY CHAPTER 8: Negativity Transformed

Negativity Transformed

Oscar was known for his negativity, and people often avoided him. He had a knack for finding the worst in every situation, and his cloudy disposition cast a dark shadow over the otherwise happy town. Each day, as Oscar sat on his porch, he watched the townspeople pass by, dreading the next day he would have to endure. His life was a never-ending cycle of pessimism, and he had all but given up on finding any joy in the world.

One sunny afternoon, a young lady named Amelia moved into the house next door. Amelia embodied positivity with a warm smile and contagious laughter that could brighten even the gloomiest days. Her spirit was unshakable, and she refused to let negativity take root in her heart. As Amelia settled into her new home, she began noticing Oscar and his perpetual frown. She made it her mission to break through his tough exterior and show him the beauty of life. Each day, she would greet him with a cheerful "Good morning, Oscar!" and offer him some homemade treats or a kind word.

At first, Oscar was skeptical, but he could not help but feel a spark of warmth deep within him. It was as if Amelia's light was slowly melting away the frosty shell that had encased his heart. He looked forward to her daily visits, and the darkness that had consumed him began to lift.

Despite Amelia's unwavering kindness, Oscar still struggled with the negativity that had become so deeply ingrained in him. He longed to be more like her, but the shadows of his past weighed heavily on his soul. Desperate for a change, Oscar turned to a higher power for help. One evening, as he knelt by his bedside, Oscar prayed earnestly to God. He poured out his heart, begging for the strength to overcome his negativity and become a light of positivity like Amelia. He asked for guidance and wisdom.

So, God sent Oscar an Angel.

One morning, when Oscar awoke, he noticed a bright light coming from his living room. Oscar got up to see what was happening, and there stood Lena. Oscar gasped. "Fear not," Lena replied. "I am an Angel sent by the Lord to help you overcome negativity." Oscar sat down on his couch and nodded his head. "God never intended for you to live a life of negativity. You allowed life and the people around you to harden your heart. God was trying to use your situations and circumstances to bring you closer to Him, but instead, you pushed Him away."

Oscar interrupted, "It's too late for me now. I'm an old man."

"Our God is a redeemer of time," Lena replied.

"But after all these years, how am I supposed to change? How can I be anything?" He questioned.

Lena smiled and said, "First, you must get in the habit of studying God's word so your mind can be transformed. Second, anytime a negative thought enters your mind, you must stop it, and this may be challenging at times. Finally, just speak life."

Oscar squinted and repeated, "Just speak life. I understand the first two. I can learn those things, but speaking life, what is that? Can I even do that?"

"Yes", Lena replied. "The words you speak have power."

Lena began teaching Oscar about the power of his tongue and words. "Speaking life and positive words are important because they align with biblical teachings and can profoundly impact both the speaker and the listener. Proverbs 18:21 says, *"Death and life are in the power of the tongue, And those who love it will eat its fruit."* The words you speak can either bring life or death, meaning that they have the power to uplift or harm others, and you will have to deal with the outcome of your words.

Ephesians 4:29 says, *"Let no corrupt word proceed out of your mouth, but what is good for necessary edification, that it may impart grace to the hearers."* You must use your words to edify and uplift others rather than tear them down.

Philippians 4:8 says, *"Finally, brethren, whatever things are true, whatever things are noble, whatever things are just, whatever things are pure, whatever things are lovely, whatever things are of good report, if there is any virtue and if there is anything praiseworthy—meditate on these things."* This verse clearly instructs you to focus on positive, life-giving thoughts and words.

Let's look at a few more scriptures. Proverbs 16:24 says, *"Pleasant words are like a honeycomb, Sweetness to the soul and health to the bones."* Gracious words not only affect the soul but also have a positive impact on the overall well-being of those around you. They can bring peace, reduce stress, and contribute to overall health. Additionally, Proverbs 15:4 says, *"A wholesome tongue is a tree of life, But perverseness in it breaks the spirit."* A gentle tongue provides life giving words that bring healing and renewal, whereas harmful words can cause emotional and spiritual damage.

Matthew 12:36-37 makes it clear that you will have to answer for your words, *"But I say to you that for every idle word men may speak, they will give account of it in the day of judgment. For by your words you will be justified, and by your words you will be condemned."* You are responsible for your speech and the moral and spiritual consequences that can arise from the words you choose to use. Therefore, you must speak thoughtfully, thinking about the impact you really want to have. Oscar, understand that your words have a lasting impact and are observed by God."

Each day, Oscar graciously and attentively took notes. He spent time reflecting and meditating on the scriptures Lena taught him day and night. As Oscar continued working with Lena, he noticed a shift in his heart. Small moments he had once overlooked now brought him happiness, and the negative thoughts that had clouded his mind slowly disappeared. He realized God had answered his prayers and guided him toward a positive life. Because of Oscar's transformation and kindness, God granted Oscar 30 more years of life. With this redeemed time, Oscar started one of the greatest positivity movements, *Speak Life Ministries*.

DALLAS'S STORY

CHAPTER 9: The Trade of Affection

Dallas spent his entire life in the shadow of a cold and distant past, a past that had shaped him into the man he was. Dallas's heart had hardened like a stone over the years, his face carved with wrinkles that spoke of unspoken sorrows. Dallas was born to two hardworking parents, Thomas and Eliza, who had dedicated their lives to their family business. They owned a bakery, which was the heart and soul of the town. Everyone would gather there to exchange gossip and laughter and, of course, to enjoy the delicious pastries that Thomas and Eliza crafted with care.

Despite their warm, inviting bakery, Thomas and Eliza had a cold demeanor regarding their personal lives. The struggles they faced in their early years, coupled with the demanding nature of their business, had molded them into distant, unaffectionate parents. They believed that providing for their family was the only expression of love that mattered, and they never quite learned how to convey their emotions in any other way.

Young Dallas yearned for the warmth and connection that seemed to flourish between the other children and their parents. He would watch his friends embrace their parents with laughter and love that was exchanged in abundance. Each night, Dallas would lie awake in his bed, his heart aching for a single gesture of love from his mother and father.

As Dallas grew older, he began to equate love with what he had observed in his parents: a transaction. He thought he would receive the love he desperately craved if he gave something valuable. This belief seeped into every aspect of his life, leaving him incapable of forming deep connections with anyone.

His relationships were fleeting and superficial, as he sought to exchange gifts, favors, and resources for what he believed was love. Dallas's life was like a hollow tree devoid of genuine warmth. As the years passed, his heart grew colder, making it harder for him to form true connections. It seemed that Dallas was fated to live an empty life.

CHAPTER 10: From Thorn to Grace

Dallas Hawthorne was a bitter and angry old man. For years, Dallas had been a successful businessman and a force to be reckoned with in his industry. He was known as a ruthless transactional leader who demanded perfection from his employees, but showed no empathy or compassion. His hardened heart had no room for love, and he went through life with a cold and callous demeanor.

One day, in the twilight of his years, Dallas encountered a preacher who spoke of the transformative power of Christ. Intrigued by the message, Dallas began to attend the small church and experienced a life-altering moment as he gave his life to Christ. With this newfound faith, Dallas yearned to change his ways and become a better person. Although Dallas wanted to change, he struggled with the discomforts his new faith brought. Being a follower of Christ stretched him in ways he was unprepared to stretch. The struggle caused Dallas to feel empty, vulnerable, and unsure of his decision. Spending most of his life in anger, he did not want to continue the trend.

One night, after all his employees went home for the evening, Dallas walked the floors of his business, reflected on his leadership over the years, and realized this would not be a change he could handle on his own. He prayed for several weeks, asking God to send him an Angel to guide him on his journey to becoming a Christ-like servant leader.

"Father God, I am seeking Your divine intervention for my transformation into a servant leader. Lord, I ask You to change my heart, open my eyes to the immense value of putting others before myself, and embrace a leadership style that is more like Your son, fostering growth, empowerment, and compassion. Let Your spirit of humility and empathy fall on me. Help me to lead with love and recognize the potential in everyone, nurturing their growth and development with unwavering commitment for the rest of my days. Send me an Angel to guide me on my journey. In Jesus name, Amen."

While working late one evening, Lena appeared in a bright light.

"Hello, Dallas; I am Lena, a messenger of God sent to help you on your journey to servant leadership."

Lena and Dallas spent countless hours together, pouring over scripture and discussing the qualities of a Christ-like servant leader. They started with Philippians 2:3-8: *"Let nothing be done through selfish ambition or conceit, but in lowliness of mind let each esteem others better than himself. Let each of you look out not only for his own interests, but also for the interests of others. Let this mind be in you which was also in Christ Jesus, who, being in the form of God, did not consider it robbery to be equal with God, but made Himself of no reputation, taking the form of a bondservant, and coming in the likeness of men. And being found in appearance as a man, He humbled Himself and became obedient to the point of death, even the death of the cross."*

Dallas's eyes widened as he remained quiet.

"To walk in servant leadership, you must have the same attitude that Christ Jesus had. Though he is the son of God, Jesus took the humble position of a servant. He humbled himself in obedience to God." Lena explained.

Lena taught Dallas the importance of humility, empathy, and putting the needs of others before his own. She guided him through passages highlighting Jesus's acts of service, showing Dallas the importance of following in Christ's footsteps. Dallas began to understand the importance of placing others' needs above his own and treating everyone with kindness and respect. Dallas's heart softened with each passing day, and he transformed from a mean and selfish person into a loving and compassionate leader.

As the days passed, Dallas appreciated the change within himself. The bitterness that once consumed him was gradually replaced by a warmth he had never known. He learned to genuinely listen, to be present, and to care for those around him. It was a slow process, but the transformation was undeniable. As Dallas's transformation continued, those around him noticed the change in his demeanor. Once fearful of his wrath, his employees now experienced a leader who encouraged them, listened to their concerns, and cared for their well-being.

Dallas continued to grow in his faith and devoted his life to serving others. He became an active church member and volunteered his time to help those in need. As he neared the end of his life, Dallas was no longer known as a mean and ruthless businessman. Instead, he left behind a legacy of love, compassion, and servant leadership, proving that even the coldest of hearts can be transformed by the love of Christ.

CLARA'S STORY CHAPTER 11: Awakening of the Prophet

Awakening of the Prophet

A woman named Clara lived in a small town nestled between the mountains and the sea. She was gifted and used her abilities as a psychic, and people from all around the region flocked to her to seek guidance and advice about their future. Clara enjoyed the fame that came with using her abilities. However, deep inside, she longed for a greater sense of purpose and connection to something beyond herself.

One day, a wandering preacher named Nathaniel arrived in town, carrying a tattered Bible and a message of hope. Nathaniel spoke of a loving God who created the universe, cared for every individual, and whose love could transform lives. Clara was intrigued by the preacher's words but remained skeptical. So, she attended one of his sermons to satisfy her curiosity. As Nathaniel spoke passionately about redemption and grace, something stirred within Clara's soul.

She felt a pull, an inexplicable longing for the divine love Nathaniel described. After the sermon, she approached Nathaniel and asked, with a racing heart, "Who is this God you speak so highly of?"

Discerning her hunger for truth, Nathaniel began teaching Clara about the Christian faith. Clara felt her heart open to the teachings. She knew it was God who was missing from her life. Not long after, she dedicated her life to Christ.

With tears streaming down her face, Clara renounced and repented for her psychic practices and embraced the Kingdom of God. Nathaniel baptized her in a nearby river, symbolizing her newfound faith and dedication to the Lord. As she emerged from the water, she felt a deep sense of peace and belonging wash over her, and she knew she had made the right choice.

As she studied the Bible more intently, she found herself drawn to the stories of prophets like Deborah and Huldah. These women had a unique calling from God, and Clara wondered if that was how God intended her to use her gifts to serve Him. Clara began to feel ashamed. She felt terrible for misusing her gift. Nathaniel had already moved on to the next town, and she did not know what to do, so she prayed a simple prayer,

*"God, please send me help. I
do not want to misuse Your gifts.
Amen"*

Moments later, God sent Lena. Clara's eyes widened as she tried to speak.

"Fear not, I am an Angel sent by the Lord," Lena said. Clara took a deep breath.

Lena continued, "God is not upset with you, Clara, and there is no need to feel ashamed. You have repented and given your life to Christ. God is proud of you and welcomes you into His family."

Clara cried tears of relief.

"Clara, God gave you your gifts to be His messenger and to help His children, not for pleasure and wealth. You are meant to be a Prophet of the Lord. Prophets are crucial to conveying God's message and guiding His people. Prophets emphasize the importance of heeding the word of the Lord to avoid consequences and maintain a close relationship with God. God makes the purpose of His prophets clear,

To receive and communicate God's message. Amos 3:7 says, "*Surely the Lord God does nothing, Unless He reveals His secret to His servants the prophets.*"

To call people to repentance and warn them of the

consequences. In Jonah 3:4-5, Jonah warned the city of Nineveh of impending destruction in forty days. The people believed God's message, and everyone, from the greatest to the least, showed their repentance by fasting and mourning.

To provide guidance and direction. In 1 Kings 22:7-8, Jehoshaphat is looking for real guidance and asks if there's a prophet of the Lord around who can give them clear direction. The king of Israel hesitates and admits that there is one prophet, Micaiah, but he always seems to bring bad news. Despite this, Jehoshaphat's request shows the importance of seeking God's guidance. It's a reminder that God's truth is valuable, even when it is challenging to hear.

To offer comfort and hope. In Isaiah 40:1-2, God speaks through the prophet Isaiah to bring comfort and hope to His people. He tells Isaiah to reassure Jerusalem that their tough times are over and their sins have been forgiven.

To tell future events and reveal God's plans. Isaiah 53:4-6 is a powerful example of how God uses His prophets to reveal what's to come. In this passage, Isaiah foretells the suffering of Jesus, who would take on humanity's weaknesses, sorrows, and sins. He was wounded and crushed so you could be healed and made whole. God uses prophecy to unveil His incredible plans.

To speak God's truth. In Ezekiel 2:7, God tells Ezekiel to deliver His messages to the people, whether they listen or not. God knows they're rebellious and might not pay attention, but Ezekiel's job was to share God's truth anyway. Prophets are called to speak God's words even when it seems no one's listening—because the message still matters.

To intercede for the people. In Exodus 32:11-14, we see Moses stepping in to intercede for the Israelites when God is angry with them. Moses reminds God of the great things He has done for His people and pleads with Him not to destroy them. He even brings up God's promises to Abraham, Isaac, and Jacob about their descendants. Moses' prayer changes God's mind, and He decides not to bring the disaster He warned about. As a leader and prophet, Moses stood in the gap for his people.

To lead by example. In Isaiah 6:8-9, Isaiah responds to God's call to be His messenger, volunteering to go and deliver a challenging message to the people, even though they may not understand or respond.

So, you see, Clara, being a Prophet of the Lord is a great responsibility." Clara prayed fervently and immersed herself in the word of God. She completely surrendered her life to God, and before long, she began to receive prophetic visions and dreams. Although excited, Clara was unsure if what she was receiving was from God, so she called on Lena.

Once more, Lena appeared. "Lena!" Clara said. "I've been having visions again, but how do I know if they are from God?" Lena responded, "If you believe you have received a prophetic vision from the Lord, here are two important things to remember: First, pray for guidance. Ask God to give you the wisdom, discernment, and understanding to interpret the vision correctly and to do what God has asked you to do with what he has shown you.

Second, test the vision. Ensure that it aligns with the teachings of the Bible and promotes love, truth, and the betterment of others. A genuine prophetic vision from the Lord does not contradict God's Word or promote evil. Remember, not all visions are necessarily from God, and it is essential to discern the source of your vision. Use prayer and the word of God. God will also send you trusted kingdom advisors to help you."

Over time, God continued to refine Clara and build her up for His purpose. Clara rose as a prophet of the Lord. She taught the word of God, spoke God's truths, led nations out of sin, and brought correction and encouragement to all of God's people.

MARIA'S STORY

CHAPTER 12: Invisible Threads

Maria Gomez was a beautiful, bright-eyed girl born into a humble family in the heart of Mexico City. She was the youngest of five siblings, with a warm and loving mother, Elena, and a hardworking father, Miguel. Maria's family lived in a small, cozy home filled with the laughter and love that comes from a close-knit family. Growing up, Maria often felt invisible. Her older siblings—Ricardo, Lourdes, Felipe, and Rosa—cast a long shadow, excelling in different areas of life.

Ricardo was a talented musician, Lourdes was a gifted artist, Felipe was an accomplished athlete, and Rosa was a brilliant student. On the other hand, Maria didn't seem to have a special something that made her stand out. Maria's family, though loving, did not have the resources or time to give her the attention she needed. Her father worked tirelessly to provide for them, and her mother was often preoccupied with caring for the other children, who had more visible needs and talents. As a result, Maria struggled to understand who she was and where she fit within her family and the world.

As she grew older, Maria began to feel the weight of her invisibility. While proud of her siblings' accomplishments, she couldn't help but feel overshadowed and unimportant. She longed for a sense of belonging and for her unique identity to be recognized and celebrated.

CHAPTER 13: Journey of the Seeker

Many find themselves lost in the chaos of the world where material possessions and fleeting trends often shape identities. Maria Gomez, a 40-year-old woman, was no exception. For years, she struggled to understand who she was, and her search led her around the world. But it wasn't until she turned to her faith that she found the answers she was looking for. Maria's life seemed perfect on the surface. She had a loving family, a successful career, and a beautiful home, but within her heart she felt a gnawing emptiness. No matter how much she accomplished or how far she traveled, it never seemed to be enough. In the quiet moments of solitude, she found herself yearning for something more.

Desperate to understand her identity, Maria turned to prayer. She asked God to guide and help her discover who she was meant to be. As the days passed, her prayers grew more fervent. Then, one day, Lena appeared. Lena, an Angel sent by God, had come to help Maria understand her identity. Lena was gentle and wise, with a radiance that seemed to emanate from her very being. She spoke to Maria with kindness and understanding. Lena helped her understand that the answers she sought could be found in the teachings of the Bible.

Together, they embarked on a journey through the scriptures, each passage shedding new light on Maria's God-given identity. "Let us begin by looking at the foundation of your identity, the moment when God created you in His image. Genesis 1:27 says, *"So God created man in His own image; in the image of God He created him; male and female He created them."* This simple yet profound truth reveals the essence of your identity. You are created in the likeness of God. God intentionally designed you to reflect His character and attributes. Maria, you are meant to be a living testimony of God's goodness, love, and grace. When you can understand and embrace your identity as an image bearer of God, you will be able to live out your purpose with confidence and joy."

Maria loved being intentionally created. Maria knew that her search was over. As they went deeper into the Word of God, Lena helped Maria to understand that she is a new creation in Christ. "2 Corinthians 5:17 says, *"Therefore, if anyone is in Christ, he is a new creation; old things have passed away; behold, all things have become new."* You are no longer bound by past mistakes, failures, or sins.

Through Christ, you are made new and will experience His freedom and redemption. Your God-given identity in Christ means that you are no longer a slave to sin. Instead, you are a beloved child of God, called to live a life of righteousness and service. As you grow in your relationship with Christ, your life will reflect His love, forgiveness, and mercy to those around you."

Scripture like Psalm 139:14 gave Maria hope. She learned that she was fearfully and wonderfully made. For the first time, Maria began to see herself not just as a product of her earthly life but as a cherished child of God. Lena guided Maria through scriptures that spoke of God's plan for her life, such as Jeremiah 29:11, *"For I know the thoughts that I think toward you, says the Lord, thoughts of peace and not of evil, to give you a future and a hope."* and Ephesians 2:10 *"For we are His workmanship, created in Christ Jesus for good works, which God prepared beforehand that we should walk in them."* Lena encouraged Maria as she continued to learn about her God-given identity. "You are not a mere accident or the product of random chance or just a child in a family. You were intentionally and lovingly formed by God Himself for a specific purpose. As God's masterpiece, you are called to embrace your unique gifts, talents, and abilities, using them to glorify God. Your true identity is found not in the world's definition of success or self-worth but in fulfilling the purpose that God has set before you."

Maria embraced her identity as a beloved child of God; she discovered a sense of purpose that transcended her earthly ambitions. Her life now centered on serving others and sharing the love of God with those around her as Maria continued to be guided by Lena. Her search for identity had led her back to her Creator, and in His presence, she found the peace and clarity she had searched for all her life. Maria knew that her journey was far from over, but now, she walked with the assurance of her God-given identity.

Maria's life changed forever after her encounter with Lena. She no longer sought validation from the world or her family. Maria knew that her identity was firmly rooted in her relationship with God. As she continued her journey, she shared her story with others, offering hope and inspiration to those who, like her, were seeking their true selves.

THOMAS'S STORY CHAPTER 14: Restored

Restored

Reverend Jacobs was well-loved by everyone, not only for his life-giving sermons but also for his gift of guiding lost souls back to the light. One day, a man named Thomas entered the church, his eyes heavy with the weight of the sorrow. He was seeking counsel and guidance, hoping to find peace in his time of need. As he approached the pastor's office, Reverend Jacob could sense Thomas's troubled spirit and welcomed him with open arms.

As Thomas shared his story, his voice quivered with emotion. He had once been a faithful follower of God, finding comfort in the scriptures and prayer. But over the years, as trials and tribulations mounted, Thomas found himself drifting further and further from the Lord. He lost his job, his marriage crumbled, and he and his son became estranged. Thomas felt broken and defeated; he could no longer see the path to healing and gave up on himself. Reverend Jacobs listened intently as his heart ached for Thomas. When Thomas finished, Reverend Jacobs took a deep breath and began to speak.

"Friend," He said gently. "I see that you are hurting, and I wish I had the perfect words to take your pain away. You've come to the right place to meet the only one who can make everything okay. God's love is boundless, and His restoration knows no limits. In the darkest of nights, God is the light."

Thomas looked up at Reverend Jacobs with tears in his eyes.

The reverend continued, "When we lose our way, it is only natural to feel hopeless and abandoned. But God is always there, waiting for us to call on him and return to Him. He is the Good Shepherd, seeking out His lost sheep, mending the broken, and healing the wounded." As Reverend Jacobs spoke, Thomas felt a flicker of hope stirring within him.

Although Thomas went to church for help, he was not ready to receive what he was asking for. Too many times, Thomas put his trust in too many people and was let down. So, he left. Reverend Jacobs could see that Thomas was on the verge of a breakdown and prayed to God,

"Father God, I come before you, knowing that even though I do not know Thomas, You know him intimately. I sense his burden and the weight he carries, and I trust that You see it, too. In your infinite mercy, I ask You, Lord, to reach out to

That night, before going to bed, Lena appeared to Thomas. Thomas could not believe his eyes.

"Fear not, I am an Angel sent by God," Lena said.

"I did not ask for an Angel," Thomas replied.

"Reverend Jacobs did, and God sent me," Lena smiled.

"Reverend Jacobs prayed that God would send you an Angel to guide you to God's restorative power."

Thomas turned away.

Lena continued, "Restoration is an integral part of your journey with God. It signifies the healing, renewal, and transformation that comes through His grace. God is a God of restoration. He promises to restore what has been lost or broken and turn your sorrow into joy. Joel 2:25-26 says, *"So I will restore to you the years that the swarming locust has eaten, The crawling locust, The consuming locust, And the chewing locust, My great army which I sent among you. You shall eat in plenty and be satisfied, And praise the name of the Lord your God, Who has dealt wondrously with you; And My people shall never be put to shame."*

Thomas turned back around, "I would not need restoration if God had never left me. He let my world fall apart."

"Listen," Lena replied, Psalm 34:18 says, *"The Lord is near to those who have a broken heart, And saves such as have a contrite spirit."* God has never left you even though you feel distant from Him. Sometimes, it can seem like God has left when everything is falling apart, but in those moments, God is working in ways you cannot see."

Thomas dropped to his knees, "I know."

Lena sat on the floor with Thomas, "The first step in the journey of restoration is acknowledging your brokenness. You are broken both emotionally and spiritually. You have faced disappointments, suffered loss, and been hurt by those around you. As you come to the realization of your brokenness, it is essential to bring your pain and sorrows to the Lord, who can heal you and make you whole again. It is only by acknowledging your brokenness that you can truly invite God's restorative power into your life.

Lena paused for a moment.

Thomas nodded his head.

She continued, "To experience true restoration, you must surrender your life to God, trusting in His plan and purpose for you. This is not a passive act. This is an intentional decision to submit your will to His, allowing Him to guide and direct your steps. It is in this act of surrender that you can open yourself up to the possibility of healing and wholeness. Do you want to surrender yourself to God?"

Thomas nodded his head.

Lena continued. "An important piece of restoration is forgiveness. You have strayed from God and blamed God for the things that have gone wrong in your life. 1 John 1:9 says, *"If we confess our sins, He is faithful and just to forgive us our sins and to cleanse us from all unrighteousness."* When you repent and turn to God, He forgives you and washes you clean. This forgiveness is a gift that will restore your relationship with Him and renew your spirit. You must trust in His ability to restore even the most challenging situations and bring forth beauty from ashes. Do you believe you can be restored?"

Thomas nodded his head.

She continued. "With restoration comes the call to help restore others. 2 Corinthians 1:3-4 says, *"Blessed be the God and Father of our Lord Jesus Christ, the Father of mercies and God of all comfort, who comforts us in all our tribulation, that we may be able to comfort those who are in any trouble, with the comfort with which we ourselves are comforted by God."* As you experience the restoration that comes through God's grace, you are called to become agents of restoration in the lives of others. You must be willing to reach out to those who are broken, be a listening ear, give a helping hand, or give a word of encouragement. You will then become the hands and feet of Jesus, bringing His healing and restoration to a hurting world. Do you want to be restored?"

"Yes," Thomas replied.

Lena wrapped her wings around Thomas and began to pray for him,

"Father God, in the name of Jesus, I come to You today with a humble heart, acknowledging Your unfailing love. I lift up Thomas to You, oh Lord, asking for Your restoring hand to be upon his life. Father, restore the areas of his life that are broken, the years that have been lost, and the hope that has faded away. Help Thomas surrender everything to You, including his pain, struggles, and desires, knowing that You are the God who restores all things. Let him see that while he may not be in control, You are sovereign, and You are always working for his good. I pray that You restore his peace, guide his thoughts, words, and actions, and realign him with the path You have prepared for him. Forgive him for the times he has wandered, for the mistakes and sins of the past, and renew his spirit with Your grace. Lord, let Your compassion and love cover him. Lord, You are the God of new beginnings, and I trust that You are already at work in Thomas's life, bringing about the restoration only You can give. In Jesus' name, I pray. Amen."

Thomas immediately felt wholeness come into his body. Through the power of God's love, Thomas found the strength to forgive himself and those who hurt him. He was able to mend the broken relationships in his life and learned to accept the past and embrace the future. Thomas was restored in faith and spirit, and he helped others to do the same. Not long after his restoration, Thomas began to lead restoration classes at the church. Lena continued to watch over Thomas and those he led back to God for restoration.

Thomas is a testament to God's ability to restore.

Warfare

God warned Pastor Terri that spiritual warfare was coming to Forever Christ-like Community Church members. He told her the members would be hit with distractions, confusion, hopelessness, panic, and emptiness. Instead of praying for more clarity on God's warning, Pastor Terri enacted church wide fasts and prayer convenings that lasted several months. She ended the convenings when she thought the spiritual warfare had come and gone. Pastor Terri and Forever Christ-like Community Church went on with life as usual.

Two years later, spiritual warfare hit after God's warning had been long forgotten. Pastor Terri started receiving phone call after phone call from members of her congregation and spiritual team. They felt hopeless, overwhelmed, and burdensome. They felt disappointment, a lack of peace, and like giving up. Minister Adams said, "I find it hard to pray. I am not sure what is going on, but I no longer want to be connected with the church, and many times I question God. Many of us struggle to trust God in areas we never struggled."

Some members felt drained. They had no energy or motivation. Others struggled with negative thoughts that brought worry and fear into their lives. Some did not see the point in maintaining a relationship with God. They wanted to go back to their old lifestyle when things seemed "less complicated." Things that people had overcome began to bring them shame. They felt like they were no longer good enough. Associate Pastor Smith admitted, "I do not feel like I fit in. I do not think I belong here anymore."

Confusion was widespread throughout the church community. Pastor Terri dropped to her knees as she remembered God's warning. She thought she understood the warning, but she didn't. Instead of getting clarity, she immediately acted, ultimately leaving everyone defenseless. She began to feel like she was no longer qualified to lead Forever Christ-like Community Church. Suddenly, doubt and fear began to flood her mind. Then she shouted, "No, Satan, you will not have my mind."

Then, Pastor Terri said a simple prayer,

> *"Lord, send us help. In Jesus name. Amen."*

Pastor Terri sat at her desk and opened her Bible.

"Ephesians 6:10-18," she heard a voice say.

Pastor Terri turned around and saw Lena. She was speechless for a moment, then turned to Ephesians 6:10-18. She read out loud. "*Finally, my brethren, be strong in the Lord and in the power of His might. Put on the whole armor of God, that you may be able to stand against the wiles of the devil. For we do not wrestle against flesh and blood, but against principalities, against powers, against the rulers of the darkness of this age, against spiritual hosts of wickedness in the heavenly places. Therefore take up the whole armor of God, that you may be able to withstand in the evil day, and having done all, to stand.*

Stand therefore, having girded your waist with truth, having put on the breastplate of righteousness, and having shod your feet with the preparation of the gospel of peace; above all, taking the shield of faith with which you will be able to quench all the fiery darts of the wicked one. And take the helmet of salvation, and the sword of the Spirit, which is the word of God; praying always with all prayer and supplication in the Spirit, being watchful to this end with all perseverance and supplication for all the saints."

Pastor Terri shook her head and cried, "This is what I should have been teaching. What have I done?"

"You still can," Lena replied.

On Sunday, Pastor Terri taught on The Armor of God.

"As believers, our challenges are not in the physical realm. We also face spiritual battles sent by the enemy to tear us away from our faith. The Apostle Paul wrote a letter to the Ephesians, a blueprint to equip believers for these spiritual battles. Apostle Paul tells us to put on the Armor of God. The Armor of God is a set of spiritual tools given to us by our Heavenly Father to protect and empower us to stand firm against the forces of darkness.

Two years ago, God warned me that the enemy would attack us. Instead of getting more clarity, I assumed that praying and fasting would be enough to prevent the enemy's attack. I was wrong, and for this, I am so sorry. I did not know when the enemy would attack or what it would look like. What's happening to us right now is spiritual warfare: not wanting to pray, negative thoughts, self-doubt, the past trying to steal our future, losing control, and feeling hopeless."

She paused and looked at the congregation.

"Ephesians 6:10-18 tells us about the Armor of God. The Belt of Truth is vital to a soldier's armor, as it holds everything in place. In our spiritual battles, the truth of God's Word holds our lives together. We need to be grounded in the truth. Being grounded in the truth allows us to recognize and combat the lies of the enemy. The Belt of Truth represents the foundation of our faith.

The Breastplate of Righteousness protects our hearts from the enemy's attacks. Righteousness refers to our upright standing with God, which is made possible through the sacrifice of Jesus Christ. It keeps us focused on our life in Christ and ensures that our hearts remain in the correct posture.

The Shoes of the Gospel of Peace means our feet must be fitted with the readiness and the peace that the gospel gives. When we walk and stand in readiness, we can still experience God's peace during battle.

The Shield of Faith is our shield against the enemy's attacks. When we trust in God and believe in His promises, we can extinguish the flaming arrows of doubt, fear, and anything else that the enemy sends our way; we can stand strong in the face of adversity and overcome any obstacles. As we strengthen our faith, we fortify our spiritual defenses."

Lena watched Pastor Terri as she taught the congregation how to equip themselves for what they were going through.

"The Helmet of Salvation protects our minds from the lies and deceptions of the enemy. By understanding and embracing our salvation in Christ, our minds cannot be shaken. The helmet of salvation is eternal security in Christ. The helmet of salvation guards our minds against doubt and despair and helps us maintain a victorious mindset. Salvation in Jesus Christ is the cornerstone of our faith, and we must guard our thoughts, focusing on our eternal hope in Christ. Philippians 4:8 encourages us to think about whatever is true, noble, right, pure, lovely, admirable, excellent, and praiseworthy.

The Sword of the Spirit is the Word of God and is our offensive weapon in spiritual warfare. By reading and meditating on the scriptures and applying them to our lives, we can stand against the enemy's attacks. Hebrews 4:12 says, *"For the word of God is living and powerful, and sharper than any two-edged sword, piercing even to the division of soul and spirit, and of joints and marrow, and is a discerner of the thoughts and intents of the heart."* It is with the Word of God that we will be able to slay all attacks of the enemy.

The last piece of the Armor of God is prayer. Prayer is our direct line of communication with God and is essential for maintaining a strong relationship with Him. Prayer is the time that you take to be one with God. Prayer allows you to be open with God. Prayer is about giving up a piece of you, and prayer is about pure communication and intentionally listening to hear God's voice."

Pastor Terri paused, took a deep breath, and looked at Lena.

Lena nodded.

"We must put on the Armor of God daily, not only while we are always going through spiritual warfare. The Armor of God equips and empowers us to face the challenges that will come to try and destroy us each day. We can stand confidently in the fact that the Almighty God protects us and that our victory in Christ is assured."

Pastor Terri continued to teach and preach on the armor of God, effectively leading Forever Christ-like Community Church through this and many other attacks.

Beloved,

First and foremost, I would like to express how deeply loved and cherished you are by God. You were created in His image, blessed with a unique blend of talents, abilities, and strengths that make you an essential part of His grand design and plan. Remember that you are never alone, even when you feel insignificant or lost. God's love and presence always surround you. It is essential to trust in God's plan for your life. At times, you may face challenges or be confronted with situations that are difficult to understand. During these moments, you must remember that God has a greater purpose for you. Place your faith in His divine wisdom, and know He will guide you through the storm, giving you the strength and resilience to emerge stronger and more steadfast in your faith.

As you walk this path, I encourage you to embrace the power of prayer. Prayer is your direct line of communication with God, a means by which you can express your gratitude, seek guidance, and share your innermost thoughts and feelings. Through prayer, you will develop a stronger connection with God and understand His will for your life. Make time each day to speak with Him and allow His wisdom and love to guide your actions. In addition to prayer, immerse yourself in the Holy *scriptures. The Bible offers invaluable guidance, insight, and inspiration to help you navigate life's challenges. Through the stories and teachings of scripture, you will come to know God's heart and learn the principles that form the foundation of a faith-filled life.*

Do not be discouraged by the temptations and distractions of this world. The path of righteousness is not always the easiest to follow, but it is the one that leads to eternal happiness and peace. Focus on God and strive to live a life that reflects Him. Be kind, forgiving, and understanding towards others, for in doing so, you will live as a true reflection of God's grace. Moreover, seek fellowship with others who share your faith. Great strength and encouragement can be found in the company of those who walk the same path. You can support and uplift one another, drawing strength from your shared experiences and learning from each other's wisdom.

Finally, remember that you are an instrument of God's love. As you grow in faith and understanding, share the joy of your journey with others. Be a symbol of light in the darkness, extending God's love, grace, and forgiveness to all who cross your path. In doing so, you will enrich your own life and touch the hearts of those around you, helping them find their way to God. Trust in God's love, embrace it, and always remember that you are a precious and cherished child of our divine Creator, God. May the light of God's love fill your heart, and may His grace guide your steps always. .

In healing,

Lena
An Angel of the Lord

Chapter 3

Psalm 51:17 The sacrifices of God are a broken spirit,
A broken and a contrite heart—These, O God, You will
not despise.

Psalm 100:4 Enter into His gates with thanksgiving,
And into His courts with praise.
Be thankful to Him, and bless His name.

1 John 1:9 If we confess our sins, He is faithful and just
to forgive us our sins and to cleanse us from all
unrighteousness.

John 14:13-14 And whatever you ask in My name, that
I will do, that the Father may be glorified in the Son. 14
If you ask anything in My name, I will do it.

Philippians 4:6 Be anxious for nothing, but in everything
by prayer and supplication, with thanksgiving, let your
requests be made known to God;

Mark 11:24 Therefore I say to you, whatever things you
ask when you pray, believe that you receive them, and
you will have them.

1 Thessalonians 5:16-18 Rejoice always, 17 pray without ceasing, 18 in everything give thanks; for this is the will of God in Christ Jesus for you.

Psalm 119:105 Your word is a lamp to my feet And a light to my path.

1 Peter 5:7 casting all your care upon Him, for He cares for you.

Psalm 94:19 In the multitude of my anxieties within me, Your comforts delight my soul.

Isaiah 41:10 Fear not, for I am with you; Be not dismayed, for I am your God. I will strengthen you, Yes, I will help you, I will uphold you with My righteous right hand.'

Matthew 6:34 Therefore do not worry about tomorrow, for tomorrow will worry about its own things. Sufficient for the day is its own trouble.

Chapter 4

Ephesians 5:31 "For this reason a man shall leave his father and mother and be joined to his wife, and the two shall become one flesh."

Ephesians 4:26-27 Be angry, and do not sin": do not let the sun go down on your wrath, 27 nor give]place to the devil.

Ecclesiastes 4:12 Though one may be overpowered by another, two can withstand him.
And a threefold cord is not quickly broken.

1 Corinthians 13:4-7 Love suffers long and is kind; love does not envy; love does not parade itself, is not puffed up; 5 does not behave rudely, does not seek its own, is not provoked, thinks no evil; 6 does not rejoice in iniquity, but rejoices in the truth; 7 bears all things, believes all things, hopes all things, endures all things. 8 Love never fails.

Colossians 3:13 bearing with one another, and forgiving one another, if anyone has a complaint against another; even as Christ forgave you, so you also must do.

Chapter 5

Colossians 3:1-17 If then you were raised with Christ, seek those things which are above, where Christ is, sitting at the right hand of God. 2 Set your mind on things above, not on things on the earth. 3 For you died, and your life is hidden with Christ in God. 4 When Christ who is our life appears, then you also will appear with Him in glory. 5 Therefore put to death your members which are on the earth: fornication, uncleanness, passion, evil desire, and covetousness, which is idolatry. 6 Because of these things the wrath of God is coming upon the sons of disobedience, 7 in which you yourselves once walked when you lived in them. 8 But now you yourselves are to put off all these: anger, wrath, malice, blasphemy, filthy language out of your mouth. 9 Do not lie to one another, since you have put off the old man with his deeds, 10 and have put on the new man who is renewed in knowledge according to the image of Him who created him, 11 where there is neither Greek nor Jew, circumcised nor uncircumcised, barbarian, Scythian, slave nor free, but Christ is all and in all. 12 Therefore, as the elect of God, holy and beloved, put on tender mercies, kindness, humility, meekness, longsuffering; 13 bearing with one another, and forgiving one another, if anyone has a complaint against another; even as Christ forgave you, so you also must do. 14 But above all these things put on love, which is the bond of perfection. 15 And let the peace of

God rule in your hearts, to which also you were called in one body; and be thankful. 16 Let the word of Christ dwell in you richly in all wisdom, teaching and admonishing one another in psalms and hymns and spiritual songs, singing with grace in your hearts to the Lord. 17 And whatever you do in word or deed, do all in the name of the Lord Jesus, giving thanks to God the Father through Him.

Chapter 7

Psalm 34:4 I sought the Lord, and He heard me, And delivered me from all my fears.

Joshua 1:9 Have I not commanded you? Be strong and of good courage; do not be afraid, nor be dismayed, for the Lord your God is with you wherever you go.

2 Timothy 1:7 For God has not given us a spirit of fear, but of power and of love and of a sound mind.

Chapter 8

Proverbs 18:21 Death and life are in the power of the tongue, And those who love it will eat its fruit.

Ephesians 4:29 Let no corrupt word proceed out of your mouth, but what is good for necessary edification, that it may impart grace to the hearers.

Philippians 4:8 Finally, brethren, whatever things are true, whatever things are noble, whatever things are just, whatever things are pure, whatever things are lovely, whatever things are of good report, if there is any virtue and if there is anything praiseworthy—meditate on these things.

Proverbs 16:24 Pleasant words are like a honeycomb, Sweetness to the soul and health to the bones.

Proverbs 15:4 A wholesome tongue is a tree of life, But perverseness in it breaks the spirit.
Matthew 12:36-37 But I say to you that for every idle word men may speak, they will give account of it in the day of judgment. 37 For by your words you will be justified, and by your words you will be condemned.

Chapter 10

Philippians 2:3-8 Let nothing be done through selfish ambition or conceit, but in lowliness of mind let each esteem others better than himself. 4 Let each of you look out not only for his own interests, but also for the interests of others. 5 Let this mind be in you which was also in Christ Jesus, 6 who, being in the form of God, did not consider it robbery to be equal with God, 7 but made Himself of no reputation, taking the form of a bondservant, and coming in the likeness of men. 8 And being found in appearance as a man, He humbled Himself and became obedient to the point of death, even the death of the cross.

Chapter 11

Amos 3:7 Surely the Lord God does nothing, Unless He reveals His secret to His servants the prophets.

Jonah 3:4-5 And Jonah began to enter the city on the first day's walk. Then he cried out and said, "Yet forty days, and Nineveh shall be overthrown!" 5 So the people of Nineveh believed God, proclaimed a fast, and put on sackcloth, from the greatest to the least of them.

1 Kings 22:7-8 And Jehoshaphat said, "Is there not still a prophet of the Lord here, that we may inquire of Him?" 8 So the king of Israel said to Jehoshaphat, "There is still one man, Micaiah the son of Imlah, by whom we may inquire of the Lord; but I hate him, because he does not prophesy good concerning me, but evil." And Jehoshaphat said, "Let not the king say such things!"

Isaiah 40:1-2 Comfort, yes, comfort My people!" Says your God. 2 "Speak comfort to Jerusalem, and cry out to her, That her warfare is ended, That her iniquity is pardoned; For she has received from the Lord's hand Double for all her sins."

Isaiah 53:4-6 Surely He has borne our griefs And carried our sorrows; Yet we esteemed Him stricken, Smitten by God, and afflicted.5 But He was wounded for our transgressions, He was bruised for our iniquities;

The chastisement for our peace was upon Him, And by His stripes we are healed. 6 All we like sheep have gone astray; We have turned, every one, to his own way; And the Lord has laid on Him the iniquity of us all.

Ezekiel 2:7 You shall speak My words to them, whether they hear or whether they refuse, for they are rebellious.

Exodus 32:11-14 Then Moses pleaded with the Lord his God, and said: "Lord, why does Your wrath burn hot against Your people whom You have brought out of the land of Egypt with great power and with a mighty hand? 12 Why should the Egyptians speak, and say, 'He brought them out to harm them, to kill them in the mountains, and to consume them from the face of the earth'? Turn from Your fierce wrath, and relent from this harm to Your people. 13 Remember Abraham, Isaac, and Israel, Your servants, to whom You swore by Your own self, and said to them, 'I will multiply your descendants as the stars of heaven; and all this land that I have spoken of I give to your descendants, and they shall inherit it forever.' " 14 So the Lord relented from the harm which He said He would do to His people.

Isaiah 6:8-9 Also I heard the voice of the Lord, saying: "Whom shall I send, And who will go for Us?" Then I said, "Here am I! Send me." 9 And He said, "Go, and tell this people: 'Keep on hearing, but do not understand; Keep on seeing, but do not perceive.'

Chapter 13

Genesis 1:27 So God created man in His own image; in the image of God He created him; male and female He created them.

2 Corinthians 5:17 Therefore, if anyone is in Christ, he is a new creation; old things have passed away; behold, all things have become new.

Psalm 139:14 I will praise You, for I am fearfully and wonderfully made; Marvelous are Your works, And that my soul knows very well.

Jeremiah 29:11For I know the thoughts that I think toward you, says the Lord, thoughts of peace and not of evil, to give you a future and a hope.

Ephesians 2:10 For we are His workmanship, created in Christ Jesus for good works, which God prepared beforehand that we should walk in them.

Chapter 14

Joel 2:25-26 "So I will restore to you the years that the swarming locust has eaten, The crawling locust, The consuming locust, And the chewing locust, My great army which I sent among you. 26 You shall eat in plenty and be satisfied, And praise the name of the Lord your God, Who has dealt wondrously with you; And My people shall never be put to shame.

Psalm 34:18 The Lord is near to those who have a broken heart, And saves such as have a contrite spirit.

2 Corinthians 1:3-4 Blessed be the God and Father of our Lord Jesus Christ, the Father of mercies and God of all comfort, 4 who comforts us in all our tribulation, that we may be able to comfort those who are in any trouble, with the comfort with which we ourselves are comforted by God.

Chapter 15

Ephesians 6:10-18 Finally, my brethren, be strong in the Lord and in the power of His might. 11 Put on the whole armor of God, that you may be able to stand against the wiles of the devil. 12 For we do not wrestle against flesh and blood, but against principalities, against powers, against the rulers of the darkness of this age, against spiritual hosts of wickedness in the heavenly places. 13 Therefore take up the whole armor of God, that you may be able to withstand in the evil day, and having done all, to stand. 14 Stand therefore, having girded your waist with truth, having put on the breastplate of righteousness, 15 and having shod your feet with the preparation of the gospel of peace; 16 above all, taking the shield of faith with which you will be able to quench all the fiery darts of the wicked one. 17 And take the helmet of salvation, and the sword of the Spirit, which is the word of God; 18 praying always with all prayer and supplication in the Spirit, being watchful to this end with all perseverance and supplication for all the saints.

Philippians 4:8 Finally, brethren, whatever things are true, whatever things are noble, whatever things are just, whatever things are pure, whatever things are lovely, whatever things are of good report, if there is any virtue and if there is anything praiseworthy—meditate on these things.

Hebrews 4:12 For the word of God is living and powerful, and sharper than any two-edged sword, piercing even to the division of soul and spirit, and of joints and marrow, and is a discerner of the thoughts and intents of the heart.

About The Author

Dr. Shavon Leach, also known as Dr. Vonie/Vonnie, is a wife and a mother. Most importantly, she is a child of the most high God. She loves the Lord and works hard daily to be more like Christ. Dr. Leach is passionate about discipleship, journal writing, and social justice. She owns Forever Open Journal & Notebook Collection.

God gave Dr. Leach the idea for Forever Open Journal & Notebook Collection to draw people closer to Him through journal writing and action. From this business came Forever Open In Christ Ministries.

Dr. Leach cares about everyone's salvation. She wants everyone to effectively live in their God-given identity and purpose, reach their God-ordained goals, and lead like Christ.

Dr. Shavon Leach wants everyone to be Forever Open In Christ!

The mission of Forever Open Journal & Notebook Collection is to give you a brave space to connect with God, reveal your inner truths, and build the internal confidence you need to become who God has called you to be so you can make your God-intended Impact.

The vision of Forever Open Journal & Notebook Collection is transformation with God's word through prayer, journal writing, and action.

Website: https://www.foreveropenjn.com
Email: foreveropenjn@gmail.com

Forever Open In Christ Ministries

Forever Open in Christ Ministries is dedicated to cultivating the transformative power of discipleship to help you live out your identity in Christ and divine purpose, set meaningful goals, and lead in every aspect of life with love.

Website:
https://www.foreveropeninchristministries.today/

Join our free community:
https://www.foreveropeninchristministries.today/forever-open-in-christ

Blog:
https://www.foreveropeninchristministries.today/blog

Angela Clemmons
Entrepreneur, Speaker, & Author
w: https://angelaclemmons.com/
e: histreasuredvessel@gmail.com

April Atkins
Prophetess, Author & Deliverance Minister
Faith Life Flow Deliverance Ministry
w: https://linktr.ee/aprilmatkins
e: faithlifeflow@gmail.com

K Angela Lee
Freedom Financial Coach
Nickel and Dime Solutions
w: https://payhip.com/NickelsDimesSolutions
e: nickelsanddimessolutions@gmail.com

Jenelle Thompson
Pastor, Founder, & Owner
Modelthat Lifestyle
w: https://www.jenellethemodel.com/
e: jenelle@jenellethemodel.com

Leteisha Tate
Coach, Mentor, & Speaker
Royal Image Coaching Consulting
w: royalimagecoachingconsulting.com
e: royalimagecoachingconsulting@gmail.com

Lissa Figgins
Christian Time Stewardship Coach for
Busy Midlife Women in Biz
w: RedeemHerTime.com
e: lissa@RedeemHerTime.com

Paul Ybarra
Coach, Pastor, & Entrepreneur
Kingdom Linked Network Inc.
w: https://www.kingdomlinkednetwork.com/
e: coachpaulybarra@gmail.com

Terrell Salley-Holliman
Health Coach, Speaker, & Author
Living Loving You Well
w: https://livinglovingyouwell.com/llyw-llc
e: terrell@tsholliman.com

Tracy Hinnant
Coach, Mentor, & Entrepreneur
Faithwalker Ministries
w: https://www.faithwalkerministries.com/
e: faithwalkerministries2020@gmail.com

www.ingramcontent.com/pod-product-compliance
Lightning Source LLC
Chambersburg PA
CBHW040832010826
48978CB00012BB/728